This book belongs to:

_____

_____

Written by Ronne Randall
Illustrated by Kristina Khrin

First published by Parragon in 2007
Parragon
Queen Street House
4 Queen Street
Bath BA1 1HE, UK

Copyright © Parragon Books Ltd 2007

ISBN 978-1-4054-9457-1

Printed in China

Mommy's Little Boy

PaRragon

Bath · New York · Singapore · Hong Kong · Cologne · Delhi · Melbourne

Robbie and his Mommy had busy days together.
Every week, they went to the supermarket for groceries.

Robbie helped Mommy put the groceries in the shopping cart.
"You're my special little helper," said Mommy, smiling.

At home, Robbie liked to help Mommy cook dinner.

He helped to set the table, too.
"My little boy is good at doing so many things!"
said Mommy.

On sunny days, Robbie and Mommy
went to the park together.

Robbie loved going on the swings,
and Mommy always gave him a push.

When Robbie said, "Push me higher!"
Mommy always did.

If Robbie ever fell and hurt himself,
Mommy always knew how to make it better.

"You're my brave little boy," Mommy said.

Sometimes, on the way home from the park,
Robbie and Mommy stopped for ice cream.

"Will I be your little boy even
if I grow bigger than you?" Robbie asked.
"Yes," said Mommy.

One day, as they were walking home, Robbie
asked Mommy,
"Will I always be your little boy?"
"Yes," said Mommy. "Always."
"Even when I am bigger?" Robbie asked.
"Yes, even when you are bigger," Mommy replied.

"I'm glad I'm your little boy,"
Robbie said.
"Me, too!" said Mommy.

"Even if I grow as big as a house?" asked Robbie.
"Even then!" said Mommy, laughing.

"What if I become a firefighter?" asked Robbie.
"Will I still be your little boy then?"

"Yes," said Mommy. "Even if you become
a firefighter, you will still be my little boy."

"I might become an astronaut," said Robbie. "Will I still be your little boy when I'm an astronaut flying to the moon?"

Zoooooom!

"Of course," said Mommy. "Even if you fly all the way to Mars, you will still be my little boy."

Robbie played in the garden all afternoon.

First he pretended he was a firefighter putting out a big fire.

Then he pretended he was an astronaut flying to Mars.

At bedtime that night, Robbie told Mommy about the games he had played.

"I was a brave firefighter," he said. "And then I was an astronaut flying through space!"

"And you are still my little boy," said Mommy, giving him a good-night kiss, "and you always will be. Sweet dreams!"